THE LAST QAHN ALIVE

UNEARTHING THE SPEAR OF NEUTRALITY

MUBARAK SANDHU

INDIA · SINGAPORE · MALAYSIA

Notion Press Media Pvt Ltd

No. 50, Chettiyar Agaram Main Road,
Vanagaram, Chennai, Tamil Nadu – 600 095

First Published by Notion Press 2021
Copyright © Mubarak Sandhu 2021
All Rights Reserved.

ISBN 978-1-63940-420-9

DISCLAIMER

The following story is purely a work of fiction and the plot is not to be associated with actual historical records. Names, characters, appearances, business, events and incidents are the products of the author's imagination. Any resemblance to actual persons, living or dead, or actual events, or with any other work of art is purely coincidental and unintentional.

AUTHOR'S NOTE

The Human Race has always been a curious one, carrying less contentment and more desires ever since it came into existence. Although this curiosity has been the driving force to uncountable inventions and advancements, the intensity of this curiosity seems to increase with time instead of fading away and bringing more sense of satisfaction in all of us.

It won't be an exaggeration of thoughts to consider this inquisitiveness of humans to be there since the very beginning; trying to be precise about this thought would be inappropriate of course. This ability to dig deep in thoughts and invent something new differentiates the minds in terms of intelligence leading to victory over one another in everyday life. Other feelings such as those of happiness, attraction, love, support and togetherness are thus shown by our loved ones while those not in good terms with us showcase envy, hatred, anger, revenge and alike.

Examples of such differences can be seen everywhere around us. If a child in class solves a problem first, he marks his intelligence thus making the teachers and friends happy attracting a lot of love and support along with arousing curiosity in some to solve other problems first in order to prove themselves more intelligent and to fetch the same praise for themselves. There are many who work out on their own, many who take some sort of support, and then, some who prefer short-cuts of copying or stealing the ideas. All of them can be observed in all professions and industries, forcing us to believe that the same must have existed centuries ago, and will remain in centuries to come as well.

I have been a deep thinker since childhood, being satisfied with a lot along with being curious for a lot more simultaneously. I used to think of the past and future and tried to bridge the gaps with my imagination. I was also fond of comparing all those virtual worlds that I used to imagine with the prevailing conditions in the present. Someone who once listened to my stories said "You seem to be just another day-dreamer initially, but your confidence and passion for life is beyond appreciation, and that can only be understood if someone listens to you for a longer duration".

At times, such words can fill anyone with enough motivation to win over the world. However, the line between confidence and overconfidence is extremely thin, and if crossed in excitement listening to such a praise, can prove to be disastrous as well. I made sure to never cross that line, and while comparing the relevant thoughts of today with the availability of resources back in times or perhaps of places with no modern resources at all, I penned this book to the best of my efforts and imaginative skills.

This would never have been possible without the support of my family and friends. This book is thus dedicated to them, as a gesture of thanks for believing in me and motivating me to enlist myself as an Author.

MUBARAK SANDHU

CHAPTER 1

God does not like to be fair. Is it because He has to offer no explanations or reasoning for his actions to anyone? Or is it just how we perceive his actions? Whole creation seems to be full of injustice and inequality. Since the first dawn, nature decided to follow God's footsteps and be unfair. While she blessed some places and made them resemble Heaven on Earth; she cursed some on the other hand, representing Hell. Uneven planes, rocky-mountains, snow-covered peaks, blazing hot deserts, barren flatlands, forests, rivers and wild oceans - all have their contrasts and their own inhabitants too who sooner or later are bound to come across each other.

In the battles away from Earth, first were the angels and the demons to clash from heaven and hell. Demons were adamant that they would seize control of heaven, while angels protected their well-deserved territory of heaven not letting it go in any possible way. In that fierce battle, one of the angels lost possession of her spear which eventually fell on earth - it was The Spear of Neutrality. The Spear was forged to destroy the cause of any battle and bring it to neutral circumstances. Ever since it was lost, peace in the heavens could not be restored. Angels and demons continued to battle, periods of peace and war circulating like day and night. The fallen angels' and demons' spirits flew downwards to Earth, seeking human form.

They had lost all memories of what they were, retaining only fragments of their nature. Over the course of their lifetime, they either strengthened that nature, or transversed into the other. Attraction of like-minded spirits grew, clans started to form, territories were being marked. Civilization had begun. However, human form was more complex than being just right or just wrong. The spirits were dispersed and as humans, they had choices to make in life. The classification of Angels and

Demons was not straightforward on Earth. There were angels among demons and demons among angels. Earth was bound to witness its very own battle too; it was inevitable.

Qahns were the first to discover the faraway Kingdom of Ekaardus. Qahns were peaceful settlers looking for new settling grounds. When they arrived in Ekaardus, it was like nothing they had ever seen before.

The lands of Ekaardus were magical. Some of the trees were able to suck gold from under the ground through their roots and bore gold leaves. Others remained laden with fruits throughout the year, housing many exotic birds and animals. The life cycles were in perfect symphony. River Nisla flowed through Ekaardus full of life and the river bed was covered with jewels visible to naked eye as the water was crystal clear. These jewels were never taken out and remained there as a part of the river bed. There was no autumn or winter that ever visited Ekaardus. It never rained either. Yet the lands sustained all the life forms. Ekaardus was surrounded by the Mountains of Vifus in the West, Forest of Clyssia in the South, White Ocean in the East and Flatlands in the North. They all had their own mysteries waiting to be explored but the spell-bounding Ekaardus never let the inhabitants leave for other locations.

Qahns were awestruck just like anyone would be seeing such an unbelievable sight for the first time. Golden and fruit laden trees, a crystal-clear river full of jewels and fish, magical weather! These lands could sustain them forever. They decided that this would be their ultimate settlement.

The leader of the Qahns, Yura, was a great mystic. He was taller than the rest of the Qahns. He looked young but he had been leading Qahns for as long as they could remember. He was the preacher of love and prosperity and promoted peaceful existence. He was above and beyond the worldly dealings but was guiding the Qahns on their journey through life. Yura knew that there must be a catch since it was all too good to be true. Yura was uneasy about Ekaardus. However, the settlement took place and Qahns started calling the Ekaardus, Home.

Yura often meditated for months in his cave and yet would magically appear whenever any of his followers was in trouble. The lands of Ekaardus provided everything, so the Qahns never had the need to be invaders. The clan was in true sense, Settled. The need for exploring comes from curiosity. What they did not realise was that the magic of Ekaardus was working on them. Ekaardus made them so content that they did not want to leave it; It eliminated curiosity by providing everything.

After many peaceful years, one day, the White Ocean turned dark grey. People went to Yura's cave to tell him about it but Yura was not there. People were getting anxious and the ocean was growing restless.

Suddenly, Yura emerged from the forest with a shining seed. He was anxious, concerned for his people, as if he knew something really bad was coming their way. For the first time, it seemed as if he was not completely prepared to face what was approaching. Still, he held his courage and quickly instructed the people of Ekaardus with his confident and loud voice.

He told everyone to run for the flatlands without any further explanation. He handed over the seed to one of them and asked him to be extremely careful with it. He instructed him to plant the seed where he felt safe. The plant that would emerge from this seed would bear leaves with the answers to the questions asked by the Qahns bloodline. All of a sudden, an army of horned-beasts appeared from the Ocean and attacked Ekaardus.

Yura knew his people were defenceless, so they had no other option but to run for their lives. He, on the other hand, tried to stop the army with his mystics. He created a shield of fire spread across the lands that the army could not penetrate, bringing down the beasts to ashes, so that his people had more time to save themselves. He shook the Earth below them in order to frighten them but that didn't work either. From within the mass of invading soldiers appeared a grey creature, human-like head and face structure but with the body of a giant crab, and crawled towards Yura. To his surprise, it went straight through his fire-shield and attacked him. Yura got distracted and the shield disappeared.

The invading army started killing the Qahns while Yura was busy fighting the strange creature. In the battle, the creature stomped over Yura with its leg piercing through Yura's abdominal portion, and it shouted in a vicious tone, that it was useless to fight the King of the Seabed, Crato.

Yura knew his end was near, so in his last attempt to save the remaining of his people, he closed his eyes and murmured the mystical formula that transformed his body into a massive force field that started engulfing everything around it. It consumed everything within its radius, including the magical power of Ekaardus. Before the force field shut itself, Crato tried to escape by forcing one of his legs out of it. He failed in his attempt and the force field shut itself breaking the tip of his leg.

Years after, civilization moved on and Ekaardus was inhabited once again. The legend of Yura and his battle with Crato was told in many kingdoms. None of the Qahns were ever to be seen again and the seed of Yura's teachings was gone with them. The only thing that kept the legend alive was that every year on the same day, the White Ocean had a grey tinge to it. Just for one day, the ocean reminded everyone of Yura's battle. Many kings and their quests failed to find the Qahns and the seed.

CHAPTER 2

Ekaardus was now ruled by King Victor who was extremely popular among all and was loved by the people of his Kingdom. He was calm, decent and humble. He never went against the spirit of Ekaardus and maintained a very positive atmosphere indeed. The Kingdom of Ekaardus was in true sense, content.

Along with the flatlands in the North, there was the Kingdom of Xiasha. Although the lands of Ekaardus did not bear any magical powers but they were still very fertile. The flatlands of Xiasha were sitting on huge deposits of diamonds, gold and silver. Kingdoms had good trade going on. The Kingdom of Xiasha was blessed with a beautiful princess whose name was Alana. She was very charming, not skinny yet not heavily built, her charming smile gave her the looks of a living angel and her blue eyes could hypnotize just anyone in the universe.

King Victor fell in love with the Princess of Xiasha, Alana. They got married and the two kingdoms were brought even closer. Together, both kingdoms stood strong. Victor adored Alana. They loved each other and their people. Few years later, Alana gave birth to a girl child who was named Zia. She was growing up to be the prettiest princess any kingdom had ever seen. As she grew older, she showed that she was not just pretty but smart and brave too. She loved horse riding and was a master swordswoman. If she wanted something, she would not rest until she got it. She had a way with people of getting them to do whatever she wanted either by her utter charm or expert negotiating skills. She would win numerous arguments with King Victor because of her quick thinking and wit.

One day, a group of nomads arrived in Ekaardus. They asked the King if they could camp somewhere in the kingdom for a few months until they were ready to move again. King

Victor allowed them to camp on a piece of land next to the Forest of Clyssia. Among the nomads, there was a young boy named Boris.

Boris was actually the adopted son of the nomad leader. He was found near a river on one of the nomad's journeys. Whether he was flowed with the water or left there by someone was not known, and didn't matter to the leader anyways as he could not leave a child abandoned there intentionally. The leader decided to adopt him and raised him like his own son. Everyone loved him. He grew up to be a man of unmatchable physique, more handsome and stronger than the rest of the boys in the pack. He came off as very distinctive to the rest of the nomads.

He was born with an unusual arrow-tip shaped vein that ran on his forehead. The 'V' made by veins was considered as a sign of victory by all and it was said that there was nothing in this world that he could not win. His green eyes and long brown hair complemented his physique. Boris was hard not to notice. He soon became a favorite among the young girls of Ekaardus while the young men envied him. It was not easy to woo him and the nomad girls already knew it. He was the one everyone wanted but no one could have. Anyways, Boris was oblivious to all this.

At Ekaardus, one of the jealous youngsters was Almus. He was the son of the Army General of Ekaardus. He was a clever and an extremely temperamental guy and his intentions to get rid of Boris were growing stronger each day as his popularity had fallen since Boris arrived. Being the son of an Army General, Almus always had an advantage of his family background and thus was used to a lot of following. Seeing that decreasing after the arrival of Boris pinched him hard. He wanted him gone by hook or by crook, but didn't know how to make it happen.

The young and beautiful princess Zia used to go out on her horse occasionally just to spend some time with nature. She was accompanied by a pack of soldiers. She used to interact with the people as well in order to make sure everyone was alright in the kingdom. One day, she wished to see how nomads were getting on in Ekaardus and rode in that direction.

Looking around, she saw Boris working away in the pack and was instantly drawn towards him. Boris looked towards the horses and saw the princess and her company. They exchanged their first glance, although a small one but a prominent one indeed. Boris bowed slightly with a smile and Zia smiled back. Even though he did not say anything, Zia felt a connection with him. It took her a while to come back to reality after seeing Boris. Almus, who always kept a watch on Zia secretly, saw this exchange and had finally got a sinister plan to get rid of Boris.

He went back to his father and manipulated his mind by conveying him about doubtful intentions of Boris. He said that Boris was playing with Princess Zia's mind and wanted to become the next King of Ekaardus by marrying her. He insisted his father to pass on the message to the King that it was in the best interests of the Kingdom to banish Boris and nomads altogether. Father, convinced to some extent, passed the message to the King. Since this news came from the General, it made a sure impact on King Victor.

He summoned Boris. Victor consulted his council beforehand and upon Boris' arrival, he was given two choices: Either go back to tell the nomads to pack up everything and leave Ekaardus or he himself goes into the Forest of Clyssia for banishment. Boris was quite surprised at this decision, unknown to what caused it. He tried to question this but there were no explanations given. One of the councilmen assured Boris that if he left Ekaardus, they would let nomads stay for as long as they wanted. They also offered free supplies for the whole time they stayed. For the sake of his people, he chose banishment, while still astounded why it was happening. As he was leaving the palace, he turned back and saw Zia entering from the other side. She was happy to see him but had no idea what had been planned for him. Boris simply smiled and carried on. Then, after walking a few steps, he saw Almus with a crooked smile on his face. Boris tried to deduce the reason for that look on Almus' face but he never had any enemy, so was unaware of what actually Almus had caused.

As he came back to his tribe, he told everyone that the King had appointed him for a special mission. He had to go into the Forest of Clyssia to find the lost chest of jewels. Boris' guardian, the nomad leader, was really upset with this sudden mission and wanted everyone to leave instead of sending him into the forest. However, Boris denied it, saying that he had already agreed to this in exchange of supplies and space for them for as long as they wanted. There were mixed responses to his action. Some were worried for his safety as the Forest was unexplored since the settlement, no one knew what hid in the dark woods. Some were happy for the security of food and shelter. Boris was sure about his decision and did not take the tribe's offer of leaving Ekaardus altogether. His people had been the happiest in this kingdom and it had been the safest they had ever been.

A few soldiers arrived after Boris. They were there to make sure Boris left for the forest and did not return. Boris walked up to them to warn them not to say anything as he had lied to his people about his banishment. The tribe gave him some food for his unknown mission. His guardian gave him a dagger that he kept for self-defence. Also, he carried a sword with him with which he always used to practice and master his skills of a warrior. He bid everyone farewell with enthusiastic facial expressions, promised that he will be back soon and entered the Forest of Clyssia.

Back in the castle in King Victor's chamber, it created unrest among Zia, Victor and Alana. Zia found out from Alana what had happened when Boris was called. Zia confronted King Victor blaming him that there was little truth in what he was told by Almus' father. Victor, on the other hand, claimed that just for the fact Zia was trying to defend a 'nobody' rather affirmed that there was something between them. At that point, Zia broke. She lamented that neither of them ever spoke to one another and only saw each other once and that one exchange caused Boris banishment. She further insisted that if it was a fault at all, then Boris was not to be blamed solely and that she was herself a culprit too. She demanded for banishment as well.

Victor got furious and locked Zia up in the castle. He gave strict instructions to Alana to keep control of her and not let her go out of the castle. Alana felt for her daughter and tried to console her. She tried to talk Zia out of her fixation for Boris. Zia, on the other hand, was adamant that she would go after him into the Forest of Clyssia. Whether Boris and Zia were destined to be together or not, but this whole incident only bolstered Zia's desire to pursue Boris.

CHAPTER 3

A mysterious man, with overgrown messy hair, arrived in the Kingdom of Xiasha asking around if anyone had seen a group of nomads. He carried a wooden staff with a crooked top. This was the piece of Crato's leg which broke and fell apart when he tried to stay out of Yura's mystical engulfing force.

He was one of the soldiers of the Seabed Army, named Taantoh, who was finding and killing the Qahns. When Yura initiated the force field and started engulfing everything around, Taantoh was the only one who had run a considerable distance chasing the innocent people of Ekaardus killing many. When he realized no other fellow-beast was around, he rushed back and could see everyone disappearing into Yura's body. Once the force field disappeared, he came back to the spot hoping Crato was victorious. He was shocked to see that the whole place had gone barren as if a giant meteor had hit Ekaardus leaving no sign of life. He found the broken piece of Crato's leg which laid right next to the spot where everyone was taken-in. He picked it up and suddenly felt a surge of energy in his body. He soon realised that Crato was not dead but confined in another dimension. He heard Crato's weak voice that asked him to find the "Seed Bearer". Taantoh evolved and transformed with time, looking more human and less beast.

The broken piece of Crato's leg gave him powers and enabled him to survive for decades and centuries, that he spent searching for the Seed Bearer. In his pursuit, he killed almost every single one of the Qahns, scattered over distant lands ever since Ekaardus was doomed. Boris and his parents were the last one left. Not overlooking the demise of all the Qahns, Boris' parents decided to leave Boris to his fate and face Taantoh. They put Boris in a bucket and prayed the river to look after him. Taantoh eventually killed them but knew that he was missing something or someone, so he carried on his search. One day, he found an empty bucket next to the riverbank. His suspicion grew. He knew that people in the kingdoms would not travel that far away from their lands. It had to be the nomads.

For many years, Taantoh travelled to distant kingdoms looking for nomads but his efforts yielded no fruitful results. Taantoh had finally arrived in Xiasha but no one had seen any nomad there too, so he made his way towards the last kingdom in that part of the planet, Ekaardus.

In Ekaardus, Zia was restless. So was Alana, seeing her daughter in such an agitated state. Alana told Zia that it was very important for her to forget about Boris. There was a reason he had been banished to the Forest of Clyssia and nowhere else. There was very little known about the Forest of Clyssia apart from the fact that they were named after a young woman named Clyssia who was believed to be the spirit of the forest. Also, nothing ever came out of the forest. Whoever entered the forest never came back either. The forest was believed to be of un-cooperative nature. No birds flew over the forest. Zia questioned more about Clyssia and the forest but Alana said that's all she knew.

In the forest, one step after another, Boris was getting deeper and deeper into the unknown nexus of trees covered with moss. As he moved deeper, he found that the trees were actually growing over giant rocks. Their moss-covered roots surrounded the rocks and eventually met the land. It was a scene he had never seen before. There were no noises. No movement. Only sounds he heard were his feet moving over the moist soil. He just kept walking and could not focus on any specific thought as the scenes around him were totally new to his eyes - unseen, undescribed and unexplainable.

While exploring the forests, the recollection of what happened in the King's Palace and why he was ordered banishment kept occurring in his mind simultaneously. Sometimes, he would remember Zia and cherish the first look which they exchanged. He would think of the moment when he saw her in the Castle and smile while moving ahead slowly. Then, he would think of the wicked smile given by Almus; this thought would boil his blood and he would start walking fast, directionless, not knowing why this happened to him and where he was going.

Suddenly, out of his thoughts, Boris felt that the trees were moving closer and surrounding him. He stood still and focussed on his surroundings to confirm what he just felt. He realized that the trees were actually closing up on him; He panicked a little, took out his dagger and started attacking them. Trees moved swiftly like a person and kept attacking Boris. He then felt a shoot tightening its grip around his neck. He used the dagger to cut it. But soon, more shoots appeared and grabbed him by his feet and arms. He lost the dagger and screamed as he applied force to break away the shoots. He struggled but the trees of Clyssia were victorious and a shoot made its way again to his neck. Boris had no defence now and was choking slowly. His vision was fading when a human figure appeared and started talking to the trees. Boris could hardly hear or see now and passed out.

He was slowly gaining consciousness and suddenly, he jumped and stood up, while still in shock. An old man comforted him by saying that he was safe now and pacified him a little. The old man said that he was not destined to be eaten by trees but rather daring adventures awaited him. He then referred to himself as the "Seed Bearer". Boris, raised by a nomad tribe, was not aware of any of these legends. They were rather simple people who just travelled for their whole life. He had just heard about the courageous leader of Qahns named Yura and no one else associated with him. So, when he was told that he was the last in the bloodline of the Qahns, it made next to no sense to him. He was brought up as a Nomad. The things that the Seed Bearer told him - Yura, Crato, Yura's plant and the Seed Bearer himself made him feel like he had actually died and was in a different world. He had a lot of questions to ask now.

CHAPTER 4

In Ekaardus, Zia kept looking at the forest from her locked-up chamber. She firmly believed that she would find Boris fair and well. She wanted to go and look out for Boris, but it was a very challenging task to break out of the castle. That night, when the young maid arrived with Zia's dinner, she thought of a plan to escape. She acted extremely disheartened in front of her and denied eating or drinking anything. When the maid insisted, Zia said she would eat on one condition that the maid accompanied her for dinner. Maid hesitated because of her status but she could not deny the princess either. She agreed. Zia demanded for more wine before they started. Maid went out of the room, locked it and returned after a while with more wine. Zia asked her to pour for both of them and she herself moved closer to the window. Maid hesitated again but gave in. As she handed Zia her chalice, Zia insisted that the maid should go first and finish the glass. As the maid raised her head to gulp the wine, Zia emptied her chalice out of the window. She repeated this until the maid was completely drunk. She then exchanged her clothes with the maid's, put her into the bed, grabbed some gold coins and managed to get out of the castle dressed as a maid.

Zia knew that it was not wise to enter the forest unprepared. She knew of an old man named Otham who lived on the outskirts of Ekaardus. Everyone thought he was a crazy old man who loved telling stories in the form of poems. He used to transform any normal conversation into a poetic one. Occasionally, he warned people of Ekaardus about Crato's return but no one believed him. People eventually got sick of him and his stories. No one paid attention to what he had to tell, so one day he decided to move away from them as he felt his words and advice were not meant for them.

Zia hoped this crazy old man would tell her something about Clyssia. She entered the market with a veil on her face and bought a horse and a sword with her coins and headed towards Otham. Otham hardly had visitors, so he was over the moon finally seeing someone at his doorstep, that too asking for his help. He welcomed her rather overwhelmingly. Zia assumed that he had not recognised her being in the maid's clothes. His cottage was full of strange things which looked more like artefacts and were definitely unique as each of them was kept with care, totally clean, having no dust on them at all. Some looked very old; others had something written on them in languages unknown to people of Ekaardus.

When Zia asked Otham about Clyssia, he had a frightened look on his face. Zia explained that it was very important for her to go into the forest. Looking at her curiosity, he started telling her about Clyssia.

"Clyssia was dishonored by her ancestors
for a minor mistake,
which she committed unintentionally of course
for no personal sake.
She crossed the line of a restricted area
and entered no man's zone,
She was forced to quit her family
and abandoned, to live alone.
Hence, she took over the forest as her home,
and dominated the trees, the waters, the loam.
She was a sad spirit
she wanted to be alone,
That's why the forest was uncooperative
unexplored and totally unknown.
Anyone who ever entered, never returned my dear

who knows they got eaten, or got burned my dear.
But, let me tell you something interesting
something you will love to hear,
If you enter for someone else, and not for a selfish reason,
Clyssia won't harm you at all, I swear."

At first, Zia was startled at Otham's poetic way of explaining everything. She then asked if Otham had ever tried to enter the forest but he replied that he had no reason. And before she asked another question, he knew what she would ask and spoke:

"No, I do not know
if anyone else tried it either.
You should also stop thinking of it
And rather take a breather".
To that, Zia questioned:
"How can you be so sure about your words? How?"
Otham answered:
"It is up to you now
To believe or not to believe,
But remember one thing
before you turn around and leave.
Your dreams can come true
if you have more courage and less flaws,
But this dream of surviving these forests
needs a very strong selfless cause."

Otham observed her for a while. As she decided to leave, Otham warned her by calling her "Princess Zia" not to enter the forest since he did not believe she had a concrete reason for the same. Zia was quite surprised to hear that. He further continued that if she was thinking she was in love, then she was mistaken. All of a sudden, the crazy old man did not sound crazy anymore.

He was stone cold serious. Zia was quiet. He continued:

"If you were in love
you would not need to ask,
Whether the forest was hostile or not
you would have just focused on your task."

It opened Zia's eyes. She realized it was yet again a case of her wanting to achieve something for her sake (She was now taught to be selfless). She bowed for Otham. She had found herself a teacher. Otham told her to go back to Ekaardus and overcome her feelings for Boris as they were not true to the core.

However, Zia had made up her mind to look out for Boris and that was the sole reason why she had fled from the Palace against King's orders. Although she was scared to go into the Forest of Clyssia, yet she couldn't resist her love for Boris and decided to go ahead even if it proved to be fatal.

Otham, with no other option left for him, handed over a shiny white metal ring to her as a lucky charm. Originally, this ring was filled with magical powers of positivity and didn't allow negative spirits to come closer than 5 metres of radius. Zia accepted it as a goodwill gesture, not knowing the eternal powers and strengths of that ring, and left Otham's place.

CHAPTER 5

Taantoh, in search of the Seed-Bearer, arrived in Ekaardus. He looked around for the settlement of nomads and found it on the outskirts near the forest. He approached the camp of nomads and enquired about their leader and asked him if he had found a baby at the riverbank. The leader sensed some trouble behind his intentions and denied finding any kid, but his expressions made it clear that he was hiding something. Taantoh asked one more time and warned him that he would kill him if he delayed the information any further. However, the leader stuck to his answer and did not tell anything about Boris. Few other men from the tribe gathered around them by now. Taantoh, filled with aggression, nailed Crato's leg into his throat and killed him on the spot. The nomads were shocked and enraged. They attacked Taantoh but he was way too powerful for any of them. Not wanting to waste his time on them, he hit the staff on ground sending a small diameter of shock wave that knocked them out, and left the place.

Now, sitting on the edge of the forest, Taantoh was drilled deep in his thoughts about how to find the last living Qahn when he saw Zia entering the forest. Taantoh was intrigued that why would someone at this time enter the forest all alone. He could not resist himself from over-thinking and thus, decided to follow her.

The spirit of Clyssia knew about more visitors in her jungle. However, neither of them was there for themselves. Zia had entered the forest solely to help Boris, if he was in trouble. She was driven by her care for Boris' wellbeing and risked her life. She was being selfless for the first time in her life. As for Taantoh, none of his actions were made for him. His purpose was to bring Crato back no matter what the cost. Clyssia had to let them in, even though their intentions were vastly different.

In another part of the forest, Boris and the Seed-Bearer carried on their conversation. Boris asked the Seed-Bearer questions about his past and his ancestors. The answers to his questions came in the form of leaves falling from the plant, which had grown from the seed given by Yura. The leaves visualized stories of his past and how his family saved his life by sacrificing their own. Now, Boris knew himself more than ever before; he was the last living soul from the race of Qahns. This realization brought a new sense of responsibility within him.

He further asked "Will Crato be back?" to which he got an answer of "Yes". Yura's force field was weakening over time as Crato, not dead but trapped, was constantly trying to break free. He sensed a responsibility to stop Crato, collected all his courage and asked one last question:

"Can I stop Crato?"

A leaf fell in front of him, he tried to find an answer from it but he found nothing at all. The blank leaf meant the answer was NO. This took him aback, feeling that Ekaardus would be finished whenever Crato returned and they were all doomed for a painful death.

Then, another leaf fell to the ground. This time, he found something really interesting and crucial in it. The leaf showed him that somewhere in the Mountains of Vifus, surrounding Ekaardus from the West, laid a spear that could kill Crato. This was the same spear that had fallen from the heavens when Angels battled Demons. This Spear of Neutrality was the only hope to get rid of Crato's unrealistic power which he would utilize to achieve his inhumane and barbaric motives.

Boris was the one destined to use that spear. Seed Bearer made him aware that he was going to enter the unexplored. If he thought that the Forest of Clyssia was mysterious, he had not seen anything yet. His journey would entail creatures and situations far beyond his imagination. Boris accepted it all and appreciated the Seed Bearer for bewaring him and set-off for the Mountains of Vifus.

On one side, Boris started his journey to find the Spear of Neutrality and on the other side, Zia continued to explore the forest in search of Boris unknown to the fact that Taantoh was following her.

Making her way through the woods without any concern of what she might have to face, Zia came across a place, which seemed less likely to be considered as just random trees. The formation of trees there, more in the shape of an amateur architect's creation, looked like a home built with walls and roofs of branches and leaves. Before she could call out for someone or perhaps knock on a door (which she couldn't see anywhere), she heard the steps of someone walking out. She tried to hide herself but whenever she tried to hide behind a tree, the tree moved away exposing her to the entrance of the Seed-Bearer's place. She had never seen a tree move; it frightened her along with the thought of someone coming out from that house. She tried to hide behind another tree but that tree moved aside too and Zia fell down on her knees this time facing the entrance.

As she tried to stand back, with her hands pushing the ground and her hair covering her face, she saw a pair of feet in front of her. Taking her eyes further up, through the minute gaps of her hair, she wanted to see whether she was confronting a human or a monster from the unexplored jungle. Before she could look up to the face, the Seed-Bearer told her that there was nothing to be afraid of and stepped ahead to help her stand up. This comforted Zia from all the wicked thoughts in her mind, although she was still prepared for something unpredictable.

The Seed-Bearer offered her some water and advised her to take a deep breath. Zia was quite convinced by now that this person meant no harm to her. Without being sure from where to begin the conversation, Zia started by introducing herself as the Princess of Ekaardus. It meant nothing to the Seed-Bearer. For him, she was just another human being but how she survived after entering the Forest of Clyssia was intriguing to him.

As soon as Zia gathered herself, she asked him about Boris.

"Why are you looking for Boris?" He asked.

"Because I care for him, and I consider myself responsible for his banishment into this forest" Zia replied.

The Seed-Bearer then told her everything that he knew about Boris and also cautioned her that the fate of Ekaardus resided in the hands of Boris. After knowing about the bloodline of Qahns and the only living Qahn "Boris" and also finding out that he was the only person who could save Ekaardus from the next inevitable attack of Crato, Zia felt even more for him but at the same time, her concern for Boris also increased as she did not want to lose him at any cost now.

There were two options for Zia – either to go after Boris on the Mountains of Vifus or go back to Ekaardus and warn the King about the emerging danger against their Kingdom. Before she could decide which option to choose, she noticed her ring shining more than usual. Taantoh had come close to the house of the Seed-Bearer and the walls of this place were hardly in a radius of 5 metres. As Taantoh started coming closer to the house, the ring started its work of keeping the harm away. The Seed-Bearer was a little away, towards the entrance while interacting with her.

Taantoh felt a push as he approached the house. He tried to move closer but he just couldn't put his foot further due to the force of the ring that Otham had given to Zia. He could not understand what was stopping him from moving further, so he started moving around the perimeter in order to see if he could find someone at the entrance of that house. To his fortune, he saw the Seed-Bearer with his back towards the entrance. Initially, he was reluctant to do anything thinking that he might lose this opportunity to gain some kind of information. However, he sensed that something was stopping him from going close to the house, so he had to pull them out in order to be successful with his sinful plans.

With an intent to attract any one from the house, he intentionally hit his foot to a rock and fell down. The Seed-Bearer saw him and walked towards him in order to enquire who he was. Just as he reached Taantoh close enough, he noticed Crato's leg in his hand. He was thrown back to the mass destruction that he witnessed many decades ago as he had seen Crato and those never-seen-before kinds of legs could never be forgotten. The way he stared at Crato's piece of leg in Taantoh's hand, Taantoh could make out that the Seed-Bearer knew about it and that he could not afford much delay in killing him.

Just when Taantoh raised his arm to drill Crato's leg into the body of the Seed-Bearer, Zia came running towards him and as she reached close enough, Taantoh was pushed back with immense force because of the power of Zia's ring. Taantoh, in a little pain, now came to know that it was something with the Princess which was keeping him away. He tried to throw a knife towards Zia but the knife fell down at some distance from her. Unknown of what was saving her by keeping Taantoh away, Zia pulled the Seed-Bearer closer to him in order to keep him safe too. But Seed-Bearer had other plans in his mind. He knew that to make the Kingdom of Ekaardus aware about the danger en route, one of them had to take the message to the King.

Taantoh was keen to get close to both of them while the Seed-Bearer tried to convince Zia to run back to Ekaardus and he would hold back Taantoh for as long as he could. Zia knew that the Seed-Bearer did not seem to be such a trained fighter to tackle a devil like Taantoh. However, the Seed-Bearer insisted her to leave by telling her that Clyssia would help him in his tough times, so he was not alone in the fight against Taantoh. This statement was strong enough to convince Zia. At this very moment, he noticed the bright shining ring on her hand and sensed something very strange about this ring. He stood up and told her that this ring was the one keeping Taantoh away till now and that she should not lose it at any cost. Knowing that this could be their last meeting, Zia thanked him and left back for the Kingdom of Ekaardus.

CHAPTER 6

Unknown to what was happening in the forest, Boris had walked a few miles out in the woods, and he started hearing a loud continuous sound of something he could not make out. As he continued walking, the sound kept increasing and he could sense that he was approaching something, about which he had a bad feeling. As his mind came up with more wicked thoughts about what he was going to face, he saw something up above the trees. It was not possible to see through the trees what was actually there, but it looked more like a huge bird. Boris tried to ignore it and moved further but the huge wings were seen more prominently this time and Boris realized that it meant danger to him.

Boris stood for a moment, took a deep breath, and all of a sudden, ran as fast as he could in order to avoid facing something he had no idea about. The swiftness of his feet covering up the distance along with the quickness of his sword which cut each branch and stem coming in its way was commendable and the bird above witnessed each move of Boris. Boris could hear those sounds very close to him now and it was almost clear to him that there was a deep waterfall somewhere very close, and the moment he realized that the sound was close enough that he might actually fall inside the waters any time, he slowed a bit in order to stop immediately if the land finished. And that's what exactly happened.

Within no time, the line of trees ended and at a mere distance of a few yards ahead, the waters flowed at unimaginable speed. No one had ever heard of such fast-paced waters in the middle of those unexplored forests; Water started from the forest and ended somewhere in the forest itself. Boris was totally exposed to the skies here with nothing covering him up from any side. Boris was trapped now, as he could not find any means to cross the waters. Then, he remembered the bird he had seen earlier and got confused as to where it disappeared.

Far away in the sky, he saw something flying as if it was playing around. The thing started coming closer, making random patterns in the air and singing something he could not understand. As it closed further, Boris noticed the patterns on its wings and realized that it was the same bird he had seen above the trees.

Boris ran in the direction opposite to that of the waters but the bird was fast enough to get close to him within a few seconds and flew right over his head making him fall down. Boris stood up and ran back in the direction of the waters this time but the bird returned again and flew so close to Boris that he could feel its claws touching his head as it crossed. The bird played with Boris just like a hunter plays with its prey. While all this was happening, the bird kept singing some tunes in its own weird way which was not actually frightening but sounded funny. Boris stopped running and stood at his place with his sword out ready to fight with this bird as it flew towards him from the front this time.

Well, another shocking incident happened which Boris could have never predicted. The bird landed in front of him a few feet away, did not attack him this time but started moving its claws to and fro along with its tunes as if it was dancing. The movement of wings acted as icing on cake to that more-of-a-dance that it was doing. Then, next moment, it stopped its movements and looked right into the eyes of Boris with no expressions at all. Boris had mixed feelings about the situation – is the bird there to kill him, shall he take the first move to attack it now, the way bird played with him showed intentions of killing him, then the dance moves and singing behaviour of the bird meant no harm, the bird standing right in front looking at him with no offensive moves, all such visions moving around in his head put him in a dilemma about what to do next.

In order to show that he meant peace, Boris put down his sword slowly and raised his arms on his sides showing his bare hands. The bird came up with another surprise when it spoke in more of a polite manner:

"Don't you speak, boy?"

Boris could not believe he actually heard that correct. Then came the next question from the bird:

"Do you even know where you are headed to, or are you lost?"

Boris tried to calm down, understood the situation and replied to the bird by telling it that he was very well aware about where he was going but the waters won't let him move ahead as he could not find a way to cross them. Further, realizing that the conversation seemed friendly, he asked the bird what its name was and why it was following him.

"My name is Bird, The Bird, that's what the trees call me. Perhaps, they are my only friends here. The reason for following will be told to you boy, once we discuss a few other things" it replied.

Boris was now almost convinced that the Bird did not intend to kill him. So, he told the Bird to ask anything that it wanted to know but also told it to be quick as he had a long way to go.

The Bird came up with a simple question;

"How will you cross the waters, boy?"

Boris had no answer to that. Further, The Bird then got a little serious and told Boris that it hardly had any questions for him and that it was just playing around. However, the play-time was over as The Bird had some important information for Boris.

"You are not alone in this Forest, boy" said the Bird. Boris asked for the details of what he was saying. The Bird first told his story that he was always there with Clyssia and the forest since ages. Any person who entered the woods with selfish motives ended up being cursed and transformed into a different species which would never be accepted by humans. The Bird, when he was young in age, developed a curiosity of going against whatever was told to him. As he was told that Forest of Clyssia was not friendly, he thought of proving the people wrong and making himself famous by going into the jungle and returning back. He had to pay for this act of his. As he entered the Forest of Clyssia, he moved in for a few minutes but then, he tried to go back as he was frightened. Well, the trees moved in front of him wherever he tried to move and he ended up running deeper inside the forest with no way of returning. After some time, he fainted out of fear and mental pressure. When he woke up, he had become this Bird and was told by a tree that if he ever tried to fly out of the boundaries of the forest, he would lose his life right there.

Boris felt much better that although he was talking to a bird, it had the soul of a human. How quickly "it" turned out to be "he" was indeed a matter of surprise. Just as The Bird finished his own story, Boris asked him about his words "you are not alone". So, The Bird said that he was watching everything from the skies how Boris entered and met the Seed-Bearer. But then, as he left, a young girl named Zia reached the Seed-Bearer's place. Before Boris could utter a single word, he further told him that she was followed by another person named Taantoh who looked quite evil. He also added that while they were talking there, the Seed-Bearer and Zia were in a fight with Taantoh.

Boris realized that the attack of Crato's army was close. A thought of returning and saving the Seed-Bearer and Zia occurred once but then, he thought of the whole kingdom in danger and decided to move further to get the Spear of Neutrality. He stood firmly looking at his sword, gaining back all the courage that he had and asked the Bird for a small favor, which was to help him reach the boundary of the forest so that he could find the Spear quickly. The Bird said that it would be too much to offer, but for the time being, he would just help him cross the waters and further, the journey must be done by Boris on his own in order to know a lot more things than just finding the Spear. Boris jumped onto the back of the Bird, he flew at a fast pace and dropped Boris off across the waters. Boris thanked The Bird, he offered further help whenever he would feel Boris needed, and Boris moved ahead.

Meanwhile, as Zia made her way towards her Kingdom, the Seed-Bearer fought with valor in order to engage Taantoh for as long as possible in order to give more time to Zia to reach the Kingdom and also to Boris to secure the Spear of Neutrality. It was easy to enter the woods, but hard to find a way out. Zia continued her efforts to return to the Kingdom in order to alert everyone while the Seed-Bearer gave all that he had to fight Taantoh, using all his strength and powers. The trees also helped him in his fight but Taantoh and the Crato's Leg seemed to dominate every move that they made.

Boris still needed one night and a day to make it to the end of the forest and another day to reach the Mountains of Vifus. He still had strength to continue moving but thought of resting for some time when the night fell. On his way, he saw some trees with huge fruits hanging on them which he had never seen before. A branch came down itself towards Boris and hung a fruit right in front of him. Boris could not make out why or how this was happening. Then, that tree told him that Clyssia was impressed with his spirit to save his Kingdom and he should consider this refreshment as a present from Clyssia herself. Boris plucked the fruit, thanked the tree and moved ahead while enjoying the delight of the fruit.

As the day started to fade off, Boris started looking for places around where he could spend some time. The darkness was emerging fast and there was nothing which Boris could light up and make his way in the darkness. Then, he saw something at a distance which looked more like a cave. He ran towards it and the entrance of the cave was quite prominently visible now. He knew that it was the perfect place to spend his night or else he would have to stay out in the trees. He jumped up the raised platform at the entrance of the cave and stepped inside where he saw some kind of dim light deep down inside. He moved inside with a lot of caution prepared to face anything coming in his way.

He never knew another surprise was waiting for him there. He heard a soft female voice quite close to him on his right "You are Boris, right?"

He tried to see through the darkness but could not find anything. He was just about to answer the question when the same voice was heard from his left this time asking for the name again. Before he could realize who exactly she was or what she wanted, the question was repeated from his back. He turned around but could not see anyone there.

He shouted loudly "Yes, I am Boris. I am Boris. Now stop playing games and tell me who you are".

She lit a few woods a little away in the cave and appeared from the other side facing the fire. The voice, that seemed to be that of a young beautiful girl, turned out to be of a creature that was partly human and partly an owl.

The creature, as seen by Boris from her feet to face was unique to its core. Long beautiful legs, slim waist, upper body covered with feathers and face – a blend of an owl and a pretty girl, with an amazing pair of eyes. Boris just sat down in disbelief with his eyes still stuck to her. He shook his head, calmed himself down and asked who she was.

She replied in her amazing voice "Klaire, that's my name. Don't worry, I am a friendly one just like The Bird you met."

Boris was shocked to know that she already knew about his meeting with The Bird. He started loving his journey now. The surprises, which initially frightened him and made his throat dry, appeared to be friendly till now and he felt good about it. Again, he wanted to know the story behind the birth of this beautiful creature named Klaire. He praised her physique first of all, pointed at her lower body and appreciated the beauty that she was blessed with in the abandoned woods. Then, he asked her about what made her half human and half owl.

Klaire offered some food to Boris and started sharing her story.

"I was a resident of the Kingdom of Xiasha. When I was an early teenager, I fell in love with a young handsome boy named Wolfey. At that time, love was not something very usual in the kingdoms. Moreover, my brother wanted me to marry his friend who was a soldier in the army of Xiasha. Both of us were not sure with whom to talk about our love-affair and that we wanted to marry each other. One day, when we were meeting at an abandoned place, we were seen by a group of shepherds and this scared us as we thought that the word about our love would be out and this might bring us a lot of trouble. Both of us decided to run and hide in the Forest of Clyssia for some time in order to save ourselves from the angry family members and the people. We never knew that such a selfish act would never be forgiven by Clyssia. After we had entered the forest for some time, we felt tired and slept out of fatigue. I only remember that when I woke up, I was alone and had no clue where Wolfey was and whether he was even alive or not. I heard someone say, perhaps one of the trees, that I was cursed to be half human and half owl forever. If I ever tried to fly out of the boundaries of the forest, I would die immediately. Therefore, I had to live here and survive somehow."

"Is that all?" Asked Boris in a confused tone, "And what about Wolfey?"

Klaire had no rigid answer for this one.

"If I was cursed and transformed partly into an owl, Wolfey's fate would have been no different. I know he is here in the forests, somewhere close. He must have missed me just like I did, he must have tried to find me just like I did, he must have cried in pain not being able to meet me just like I did. The trees here hide something from me as if not telling me about Wolfey is also a part of my curse. Whatever be the situation Boris, I know I am going to find Wolfey one day for sure, and living with him till my last breath now would be a pleasure worth dying for."

Boris listened to her sentiments quietly, did not react much to what she said for some time, and then just walked off towards the entrance of the cave. Looking at the darkness outside, Boris started thinking for reasons of meeting all the people in the forest but could not find one particular logical assumption which he could consider to be appropriate.

Cool breeze accompanied him along with a blend of noises emerging from the woods. He could hardly see anything except a few trees but could expect bundles of more surprises and adventures waiting for him the next day.

"You should sleep." Klaire advised Boris. "A long day waits for you. Make sure you give yourself some rest before facing it". Klaire pointed towards a bed-shaped long branch covered with leaves and told him that he would not find a better place to rest in an isolated cave in a jungle.

The next day, Boris felt fresh, energetic and ready to encounter more surprises. Klaire did not speak much, just kept looking at Boris wanting him to stay a little longer because it was after a long time that she had met a human out in those forests. However, she did not tell that to him, as she knew he had to move on with no other alternative available.

Boris was fascinated about everything he faced in the forest. He was always sure about his confidence and courage but never knew it would lead him to such a moment that he would risk his own life to save the Kingdom of Ekaardus.

With his thoughts still running around in his mind, he thanked Klaire for being so kind to him. He further assured her that on his way through the woods, he would also keep an eye around and see if he could find Wolfey and if he did, he would tell him about Klaire and that she still waits for him.

With a touching tone to his words and intense eyes filled with respect, he raised his hand to bid goodbye to his new friend, the ever-gorgeous and charming, Klaire, not knowing whether they would ever meet again or not.

Back at the Seed-Bearer's place, the fight intensified as Taantoh could not be defeated and didn't back out as well. But slowly, as a part of his strategy, he was moving backwards while fighting, with a plan to move back towards the Kingdom as it was not easy to win over the Forest Trees and the Seed-Bearer together.

By this time, Zia also managed to find a way out of the forest. The news of Zia entering the Forest of Clyssia had spread like wildfire already, and now that she had returned out of it, left people stunned, as they had never heard of anyone coming out of the Forest of Clyssia. She ran towards the King's Palace awaring everyone in her way about the fierce war coming towards them and to prepare for the worst. She also saw Almus but avoided him for now, thinking about dealing with him later.

CHAPTER 7

Boris continued his journey in the woods and moved ahead making his way through the grass and branches. Initially, for some distance, he ran at a considerable pace in order to reach his destination quickly. Then, he thought he might lose too much energy in running and won't have much time to respond if any danger came up, so he started walking. More than an hour passed and he did not come across anything that could be considered unpredictable.

His happiness for this calm start to the day was just increasing when he sensed something following him. He did not turn back suddenly, nor did he change the pace with which he was walking. He just held his sword firmly and prepared himself to encounter just anything in his way.

"Come on, show yourself, come on". He kept murmuring to himself while moving ahead carefully.

As he went past a few more trees, in front of him stood three wolves. They looked hungry, really hungry. The way they looked into the eyes of Boris, anyone would faint out of fear but Boris just stuck to his ground and gripped his sword more firmly. Boris was confident to win over them, not easily, but definitely.

The wolves started closing their distance, Boris moved ahead as well to exhibit his courage and to show that he was not frightened. Standing a few feet apart and facing each other, all of them were filled with aggression to kill and win. The wolves spread out in order to attack Boris from different directions. Boris moved towards a tree with an extremely wide trunk as a strategy to save himself from an attack to his back.

In a blink of an eye, one of the wolves jumped onto Boris. The leap was quick, but not quick enough to catch Boris by surprise. He rolled away keeping his eyes on all three wolves. He waited for another attempt by the wolves which came in a hush again. All three of them jumped together towards Boris. He ran towards one of them and managed to mutilate it while bending down as it was still in the air. This swift move by Boris left an impact on the wolves and they backed off a bit in a dilemma to attack him again or run away.

However, in an unlikely manner, the wolves started moving back even though Boris showed no gesture of attacking further. He just stood in a defensive stance to save himself expecting them to attack again. But they kept moving back slowly for some distance and then disappeared in the woods. Boris had a strange feeling about this sudden change in their behaviour. He was not a person who would just enjoy an easy victory, he would think deep into the matter to consider various possibilities. Then, it just struck his mind, that maybe, for once, he should look back too!

The tree behind him had a huge trunk which took the shape of a 'Y' at a height of approximately 15 feet. In the middle of the trunk, where it divided into two halves, stood another wolf.

Yes, it was a wolf, but no, not just any other wolf. The size of the wolf was considerably huge and its unmatchable strength was crystal-clear from its muscular structure. Silver fur all over its body shined bright in the daylight. As was clear from its appearance, the Silver Wolf could not be taken over as lightly as the other wolves. Also, the Silver Wolf was the reason why other wolves ran away. Boris knew it now, and prepared himself for a tougher fight. However, there was not a single sign of attack from the Silver Wolf. It just stood there and looked at Boris.

"What now haan?" whispered Boris looking at the Silver Wolf.

"What now?" He spoke a little loudly this time, loud enough to be heard by the Silver Wolf.

"For now, you get to live" spoke the Silver Wolf in a heavy voice, just like a dictator talks to the people under his command.

"Oh, so now you speak too?" said Boris "And may I know the reason why I get to live? Don't you feel like eating me up just like the other wolves?"

The Silver Wolf seemed a bit annoyed about being compared to the other wolves. He jumped down from the tree right in front of Boris and stood next to him. Boris still had his sword ready to save himself in case the Silver Wolf attacked.

"Well kid, first of all, don't you dare compare me with those cowards. And the next thing, which should interest you more, is that I have come across a human after a very long time. I won't harm you. There must be a very solid reason why you are here in these forests, that too in the human form unchanged. Let's have a word about it."

"After a very long time?" Boris asked. "When was the last time you saw a human by the way?"

The Silver Wolf turned away on this question as if it did not want to answer. By now, it's strong sturdy body language was not strong any more. It took a few steps away from Boris with its eyes numb just like a person gets emotional on remembering something and feels like spending some time in isolation.

Boris lowered his sword and asked the Silver Wolf to stop and talk to him. He did not want to abandon it as he had started believing that it was another friendly animal just like The Bird and Klaire. Boris tried to insist the Silver Wolf to tell him why it suddenly moved into a state of demise. The Silver Wolf stopped, looked towards Boris and took a long breath before speaking the most unexpected words.

"The last time I saw a human being, she was in my arms and we slept together out of fatigue. When I woke up, she was gone."

Boris was awestruck after what he heard, and was almost into tears. He stood still like a statue, trying to believe what he heard was actually real and not a misconception. The words of Silver Wolf pointed towards Klaire. Boris was sure there could be no one else matching that situation and just one statement made him so anxious to listen more that he couldn't resist from shouting out the name "Klaire".

"Klaire! Was she the one whom you met last?"

It was the Silver Wolf's turn to respond in disbelief now.

"What did you just say? Did I hear you right? Did you really utter the same name that I just heard?"

Getting over the feelings of shock, a wave of happiness hit both of them and the expressions of joy started emerging on their faces. Slowly and gradually, they could read a sense of happiness in each other's eyes and both waited for the other one to say something out of joy. Once again, "it" turned out to be "he", totally opposite to the appearance of a wild animal, just like The Bird earlier.

Then, Boris spoke:

"Wolfey is your name and you came here with Klaire in order to hide, scared to be caught by the people of your kingdom. You were too tired to keep moving, so you relaxed, eventually slept and never saw Klaire again when you woke up. Right?"

There was no one else who knew about it except Wolfey and Klaire as they were the only ones out there when everything happened. Therefore, it was clear to the Silver Wolf that if Boris knew their story, it was told to him by Klaire herself and no one else.

"Tell me where you met Klaire, tell me right now and I will do anything for you in return" said the Silver Wolf with a hope to meet his parted soul very soon.

Boris had nothing to ask for but had a lot to tell. So, he told the Silver Wolf about his journey in the forest, his meeting with the Seed-Bearer, The Bird and then, Klaire. He told him that she still looked fabulous and had the most beautiful voice he had ever heard. Her appearance of an owl was also told by Boris to the Silver Wolf. The Silver Wolf had no other option but to regret his decision of entering the forest. However, that also revealed their never-ending love for each other for which he was glad too.

"Crato must be close to getting free, I must hurry" Boris spoke to himself looking towards the Sun, realizing almost half the day had already passed and he had yet to cover a lot of distance.

"Crato? What are you saying? I have heard the stories of Yura defeating Crato in the most memorable battle of Ekaardus. He is dead. Are you expecting the deceased back into this world?"

The Silver Wolf was a little sarcastic making this statement but somewhere in his mind, he wanted to know more from Boris because if Boris was there in the forest alone, there had to be a very solid reason behind it.

Boris then explained to him everything he was told by the Seed-Bearer. Knowing that Boris was the last living Qahn, the Silver Wolf respected him even more as the Qahns were remembered as the race of Yura, who won over a vicious army alone. Further, the Silver Wolf told Boris that it would take him quite long to reach the Mountains of Vifus; it would be better if Boris could sit over his back and he would take him to the end of the Forest of Clyssia, that was the last point where he was permitted to go.

Boris appreciated his kind gesture of offering him the ride. He knew it was going to be the most uncomfortable ride he would ever have in his life, but there was no better option to finish his journey quickly. Without wasting any more time, he jumped on to the back of the Silver Wolf, held firmly to his shining silver fur, and asked him to start-off immediately.

The Silver Wolf ran at an unbelievable pace, jumping over the rocks and running past the beautiful sceneries wherein Boris could see the sun rays cutting into the forest through the dense leaves and branches. While he ran, all his focus was to take Boris to the boundary of forest at the earliest, and come back to meet Klaire. Thoughts of meeting Klaire took him so bad that he didn't even realize he reached the edge of the forest and was about to exit the forest when Boris shouted loudly.

"Stop. Stop, or you won't live to see Klaire."

All of a sudden, the Silver Wolf stopped, still not completely out of his thoughts. Then, he saw a row of just a few more trees ahead which needed just one more leap for him to cross. He thanked Boris for telling him to stop or he would have died without meeting his love.

Boris told him about the location of Klaire's cave and to be with her forever. Sharing no more words, Boris just raised his hand to say goodbye to another friend that he earned during his journey. The Silver Wolf nodded his head, turned back towards the forest and disappeared into the woods in no time. Boris stepped out of the forest and headed towards the Mountains feeling a great sense of responsibility towards the Kingdom of Ekaardus.

As the Mountains started to appear, Boris' excitement to find the Spear of Neutrality grew but where to look for the Spear in the vast area of Mountains was something he had no clue about.

There was no way he could move ahead without any rigid plan, so he thought of all the people he met and the things that happened in order to extract some fruitful ideas out of them. His thoughts took him back to the moment when his questions were being answered by the falling leaves. The visuals of the Spear of Neutrality made it very clear how the Spear looked like but its location was still blurry. Then, he remembered the trees surrounding the Spear. Further, he could recall a chain of mountains surrounding this group of trees.

"Yes, yes, that's where it has to be. That's how the whole vision started and led to the Spear. It all started from the top. In the middle of the Mountains of Vifus, they form a circular shape surrounding an unpredictable depth of darkness. Deep inside grow magical unseen trees; covered by the roots and moss lies the Spear of Neutrality somewhere in this area, which shines bright and can be noticed from a considerable distance. Yes, that's what I visualized and that's where I need to go. Come on Boris, you can do it, come on." Boris recalled everything, encouraged himself and moved ahead towards the middle of the mountains.

Walking through the mountains for a couple of hours and climbing up the steep slopes, he did not realize how high he had come and reached an edge at the top of a mountain. He thought of moving along the edge when he just looked around for a while. There was a smile on his face as he looked around. Peeping below, he could not see anything but darkness of the depths. The darkness was surrounded by huge mountain cliffs and Boris was standing on one of them. This was exactly the location he was looking for. Now, he had to find his way down before the sunset.

From nowhere, he heard a voice:

"Move on, son, for it's already too late to wait and think."

Again, as a measure of safety, Boris took out his sword and stood in a stance ready to face any sort of danger. Holding himself to his position, he just moved his eyes around to see if he could find anyone. He couldn't see anyone, so he just questioned:

"Who are you? And, well, where are you?"

"You know me. Not my voice, not my appearance, but my name." The voice answered.

Boris: "Do you mind telling your name then, wherever you are?"

"Yura", he said.

For a few seconds, Boris was taken back to everything told by the Seed Bearer and the heroic stories of Yura, whose bloodline was now being carried forward by him alone. Then, out of his thoughts and back into reality, he quickly put his sword back and looked up towards the sky. He could sense the voice coming from up there but could not see anyone.

"Yura! The one whose powers are still remembered by all, who saved the Kingdom of Ekaardus alone, the leader of Qahns, Yura." Boris bowed down in respect.

"Stand up my son, I saved Ekaardus then but it's your turn to be the savior now."

Boris felt lucky to be interacting with the one whose legendary tales were popular among all but whom no one had ever met. But it was not the right time to let his excitement overweigh the sense of responsibility, so he stood back and asked for the fastest way to the Spear and also, back to Ekaardus. The answer that he got left him confused whether he should go ahead with it or not.

"The fastest way down to the spear is by jumping down into the depths, the fastest way back up is to jump up with all the force you have got, but the only way to move back to Ekaardus is to take the same path that you took to reach here."

Boris looked down into the depths to see if he could find anything that he could hold if he jumped, kept looking for a while but couldn't see anything except darkness. He looked back towards the sky and asked if there was any other alternative.

"You have never seeked alternatives in your entire life. Why now?"

Those words were enough to encourage Boris to jump with no thoughts of what would happen next. Standing right on the edge with his back towards the depths, he looked up, spoke in an assertive voice "Amen" and let his body fall in the depths while still staring at the skies with his eyes wide open. He kept falling for some time before he felt his pace slowing down as if something was stopping him from falling. Next, he saw small birds flying around him chirping and singing their own rhymes. They were more majestic and beautiful than he could ever imagine a bird to be. They formed a support-base under Boris and took him down towards the ground. On reaching the top of the trees, the birds flew away leaving Boris on a long wide branch of a tree with shining white leaves and golden flowers. Boris sat on his knees and watched the magic happening in front of his eyes. The branch bent below slowly taking Boris close to the ground and he jumped off as soon as the branch halted. He was surrounded by those beautiful glittering trees with white leaves and golden flowers.

Just when he stopped looking around and looked straight ahead of him, at a distance of approximately 50 yards, he could see a bright yellow light coming off a shining object. As he walked close, merely a few feet away from him, the shine got brighter and he could feel its power embracing his presence.

As he moved closer, his instincts confused him at each step as he had faced a lot of hardships lately and getting hold of the Spear of Neutrality could not be a piece of cake without emergence of another trouble, he believed. As he moved, he kept an eye on the surroundings to be prepared in case anything appeared out of the blue.

He went closer, cleared the moss, pulled the branches away, and saw the Spear of Neutrality lying in front of him. Just by the look of it, he could make out it was not something designed or created by humans; the Spear of Angels had a very unique appearance and a stronger feel to it. He bent down, held it with both hands and felt a wave of strength in his body as if he was hit by a superpower.

He was exactly half-way through his journey. He closed his eyes and thanked the almighty for all the learnings and strength that he was blessed with during the past couple of days. Still in disbelief that he had got hold of the Spear of Neutrality, he looked around at the magical scenes of beauty once again before returning back.

CHAPTER 8

Holding the Spear firmly, with all the strength he had, he pushed the ground below him so hard that it shook the trees around him and he jumped as hard as he could in order to reach the top of the mountains in a single leap, as was told to him by Yura. He enjoyed moving up through those fabulous trees and the pretty little adorable birds. Further up, he noticed the darkness growing below him as he was getting away from that place and moving close to the mountain peaks. His jump took him back to the same spot from where he had fallen. He rolled and landed on the ground and made sure he had his sword and the Spear with him. On checking everything, he looked up to see if he could still find someone up there or hear Yura's voice once again. However, that was not supposed to happen. Holding the Spear in his left hand and wearing the sword and the dagger hanging by straps to his waist, he started back where he had come from.

He moved swiftly in order to cover up as much distance as he could before sunset. At times, he would run fast and at times, he would jog or walk conserving his energy for another sprint. Just before sunset, he reached the Forest of Clyssia.

As he entered the forest, to his surprise, the Silver Wolf stood in front of him waiting for his return as he knew that Boris would take the same path to return to Ekaardus. He welcomed Boris back to the forest and offered Boris to ride him once again.

First, Boris thanked him for coming back, then he told him about his successful attempt of finding the Spear and then showed him the Spear as well. With no questions to ask and a lot more still to share, Boris jumped on to his back and asked him to run as fast as he could. Boris thought that Silver Wolf would take him to the other part of the forest. However, Silver Wolf had something else in his mind. The Silver Wolf, or to call him

Wolfey, ran faster than earlier and just before the darkness could rule the night, he reached Klaire's cave.

Boris could not wait to see the lovers together and that was, more or less, possible because of him only. As both of them entered the cave, Wolfey called out for Klaire.

"Come my love, what took you so long?" Klaire asked in her beautiful voice.

"He got late because of me" spoke Boris before the Wolfey could even think of breaking the surprise.

Klaire was overwhelmed on seeing Boris. She walked over to him, looked straight into his eyes and thanked him for helping her meet Wolfey. It could not have been possible had Boris not travelled through the forest.

Boris showed her the Spear of Neutrality and just when he talked about it, Klaire got serious as if she recalled something that she had to tell. Boris realized it as well, and waited for Klaire to say something. When she didn't break the silence, he stared at Wolfey and waited for him to say something. Just when he was about to insist both of them, Klaire spoke:

"The attack on Ekaardus has begun."

These words brought a shock-wave to Boris and stopped his breath for a moment. The time was flying and he could do nothing but to keep patience and continue his journey back to Ekaardus. Clarity about the intensity of attack and the kind of attacking army was of utmost importance in order to prepare himself accordingly. He asked Klaire and Wolfey to tell in detail what all they knew about the attack.

Klaire tried to speak in her disheartening voice but broke down. Wolfey explained:

"Zia was able to make it back to the Kingdom and convey to the King everything she was told by the Seed-Bearer and her encounter with Taantoh. The King did not ignore a single word spoken by her, and told the Army General to prepare his soldiers for the toughest battle of lifetime.

The Seed-Bearer and the trees of Clyssia fought against Taantoh for a long time. Just when he seemed to be backing off and nearing defeat, he changed his fighting patterns and escaped the face-off as if it was a part of his plan as well. He engaged the Seed-Bearer and the forest in a fight of his own, while the legendary Yura got his focus on the last living Qahn (pointing towards Boris). This was a perfect time for Crato to escape the dimension that he was held back in; he gave everything that he could from inside while Taantoh did his part from the outside."

He continued further:

"The moment Taantoh escaped the Forest of Clyssia, he headed straight for the Ocean. And yet again, just like we heard the stories of Crato's first attack, the waters of White Ocean turned dark grey. The only difference this time was that their army had a soldier standing on the outside waiting for them."

Boris could not stop himself and interrupted Wolfey with a few of his own questions:

"How do you know all this? Why didn't Clyssia or you join the fight against Taantoh when you all knew he was the wrong one? Is the Seed-Bearer still alive? Is the attacking army being led by Crato right now, or by Taantoh for the time being? Please tell me everything quickly, please."

Klaire could feel his emotions and tears never stopped coming out of her eyes. Wolfey calmed Boris down and assured him that he would answer all the questions. Boris' blood was boiling, how could he calm down when his people were in danger of being killed by the merciless army of Crato. He insisted Wolfey to answer quickly, or he would leave without listening.

Wolfey started speaking hurriedly this time:

"We know all this because the trees of Clyssia act as messengers for every new development taking place in and around the forest. The word is shared and spread within no time. Taantoh was fought against collectively by Seed-Bearer and the trees but Crato's leg provided him immense strength which helped him fulfil his motives and get away. We, the creatures of this forest, can only fight on Clyssia's word. And believe me when I say it, such things do not happen every other day and decisions for the same are never pre-planned or easy. Clyssia is sad for not being able to help, and in fact, all of us are sad about this altogether. Talking about Seed-Bearer, oh yes he is alive and fine and perhaps waiting for you to return with the Spear of Neutrality. Last, but the most important one, Crato's army is being led by Taantoh for now. Crato may appear any time, and if you don't stop him, Ekaardus may not survive his wrath."

Boris looked into the eyes of both Wolfey and Klaire, nodded his head in appreciation of everything done and told by them, and ran out of the cave to return to his land irrespective of the falling night. As he reached the waters flowing swiftly between the forest, The Bird was already waiting for him there; well, Boris was not surprised this time as he already anticipated him to be there for his assistance. Without any question or delay, he jumped on to the back of The Bird and asked him to fly. The Bird knew the rush, didn't exchange any word during this flight and dropped him off near the Seed-Bearer's place from a considerable height testing Boris' strength to jump and land, perhaps another lesson to be learnt before going for the battle. Boris managed to touch down safely and didn't even realize how easily he did all that, as all his concentration was on reaching back.

He reached out to the Seed-Bearer who was preparing himself for a tougher fight than he had with Taantoh some time back.

"It feels good to see you with the Spear" Seed-Bearer said. "I have some weapons of my own if you don't mind me accompanying you".

"There's not enough time to stay and talk; Let's move." While saying these words, Boris ran towards Ekaardus. The trees helped Seed-Bearer to cope up with Boris, by moving him ahead with the help of branches. Seed-Bearer would just sit on a branch while the tree extended it to the next one. The whole forest was impressed by the zeal and strength of Boris. Clyssia, perhaps, was more impressed than the rest.

CHAPTER 9

Back at the lands, the Kingdoms of Ekaardus and Xiasha stood together against the vicious army of Crato. Just like Wolfey told Boris, Crato's army made its way out of the Ocean and followed Taantoh for the attack. As Taantoh led them towards the Kingdom of Ekaardus, he could feel the energy in Crato's leg getting stronger, further making him feel more energetic and aggressive, perhaps more barbaric.

King Victor knew that his armies would not be able to defeat Crato, Taantoh and all the invading aggressors. They could just buy some time for Boris to return and help them get through this battle alive. All the residents of Ekaardus just prayed to God for all kinds of help that could be provided; the prayers for early return of Boris dominated all others.

It was now time for the final face-off. The soldiers of Ekaardus and Xiasha, covered the way leading towards the Kingdom of Ekaardus. Taantoh was now visible to all, leading the army of ruthless beasts, carrying some sort of long sharp-edged weapons. The sound of their feet hitting the ground scared the hearts out of everyone, yet the soldiers held their stance prepared to die for their motherlands. Another thing which was equally scary was that Taantoh and the beasts didn't slow down or gather pace while marching towards them. They moved at a constant pace as if they were hardly bothered about the soldiers of Ekaardus. The Army General, standing in front of his men, showed great valor by keeping his patience and waiting for the right time to charge.

King Victor, Queen Alana and Princess Zia stayed back inside the King's Palace and gathered the people of their Kingdom inside. Some men, along with the King himself, guarded the castle to keep the invaders away. Almus was nowhere to be seen, neither with the fighting soldiers nor with the people in the palace.

Taantoh had now come face-to-face with the Army General. Although the General did not expect any exchange of words at the moment, yet was open for talks in case Taantoh spoke, and he actually did!

"General Oh General, can you see death knocking the doors oh General?" Said Taantoh in a scary rough tone.

General had no answers. He tried to hide the fear inside, didn't shiver but didn't respond strongly either. His eyes spoke a lot though.

"You really think you can stop us General?" Said Taantoh again.

General looked at him, didn't blink at all, kept his cool, and asked:

"What brings you here?"

Taantoh responded with an evil laughter first, looked back towards his army next, looked back into the eyes of General again and said:

"Everyone wants to be at the best place and have the best lands and rule the best kingdoms. We can win over any land and live anywhere General, but you see, this kingdom is the best out there, and nothing better has ever been heard of. And well, we don't want our armies to start from scrap. There will be a time when we will rule the world, but once we erase you all from this land, the message of our victory will spread strong, very strong. And our terror will grow by leaps and bounds, in kingdoms and provinces, no matter big and small. And no one, General, no one, will even dream of defeating us. We won't have to face people like you who stand against us then, the moment they will see us, they will quit their stand then and there. That's why we start from the strongest kingdom and the strongest army, General."

General obviously knew that there was no scope of any sort of negotiation, but this level of brutality and barbarism only got clear to him at that specific moment and it shook him from within leaving all the battle tactics and strategies behind.

"And one more thing, General" Taantoh continued," Our invasion was interrupted by Yura earlier, and we are well aware that his bloodline has still not ended. I don't expect that Qahn will return and fight for you all just like Yura did, but if he does come back, it will be one of my most seeked moments when I kill him myself along with all of you".

As soon as he finished speaking, his beasts started moving forward towards the army of Ekaardus. The General raised his sword and told his soldiers to fight strong till their last breath.

And the battle began.

While the General instructed his soldiers to fight in the battle formation, the beasts followed no strategy but to attack and kill. Those merciless ones were undoubtedly stronger than the human power, but the soldiers were more in number which gave them enough strength to hold back the invaders. Also, the tightly packed soldiers did not counter the beasts with power alone, but with the war tactics of safeguarding themselves with the shields while piercing them with the spears through the shields as is practiced by any warrior.

On the other hand, the General faced the aggression of Taantoh alone mainly to keep him away from the battle as he knew the Crato's leg gave immense power to Taantoh which could not be tackled by his soldiers. Crato's leg was the reason why Taantoh overweighed the General and his soldiers who tried to attack him. General even tried to get closer and catch hold of that leg from Taantoh but failed in his attempt to do so.

Just when the General and his army gained enough confidence that they could defeat Taantoh and the ruthless beasts, the ocean tides grew larger than ever and the earth quivered. It scared every human soul fighting for their lives out there, but hardly bothered the invaders.

Something jumped out of the waters magically high towards the sky and for a few seconds, each weapon in the battlefield stopped. The soldiers of Ekaardus and Xiasha were stunned, the beasts stood still and each eye looked up in dilemma as to what was going to come next. And within no time, it landed back in the middle of the war-ground.

Stronger than before, exasperated and fierce, in the middle of everyone, stood the King of Seabed - Crato.

CHAPTER 10

Crato's presence took everyone by storm; while the soldiers and the General could sense their deteriorating chances of survival, Taantoh and the beasts knew they were going to win over the Kingdom very soon. The beasts gathered back around their King, Taantoh moved closer to him and raised Crato's leg up towards the point from where it had broken. The leg got connected back to Crato with immense force and lightning.

On the other hand, General quietly moved back his army in formation again and pointed towards the beasts instructing his soldiers to fight them only, instead of focussing on Crato or Taantoh. He knew they had no chance against them both; it would only be better if he continued tackling Taantoh, especially when Crato's leg was no more in his possession, and if his soldiers kept stopping the army of beasts. Crato could not be stopped by either of them, neither individually nor together.

Crato ordered Taantoh to finish off the General at the earliest and follow him to the King's Palace as that was where the King's family was, and they were the ones whom he had to kill in order to conquer the kingdom.

Taantoh bowed down to Crato, nodded his head in response, and shouted at his army to kill each living resident of Ekaardus and Xiasha or die themselves. The battle that had stopped for some time, started more fiercely this time with each soldier screaming out loud at the offence and hitting harder with all the force and energy they were left with.

While the beasts kept fighting the soldiers, and Taantoh continued his fight with the General, Crato headed towards the King's Palace straight away, easily killing anyone coming in his way. Just when he saw the palace, he noticed King Victor, Queen Alana and Princess Zia leading the people and guiding them in order to keep them safe. This made him even more aggressive as his presence had not shaken the kingdom as he had expected. He assumed all the plans and strategies to go haywire, but seeing the opposite made him belligerent.

From a considerable distance, he raised his front two legs and shot something out of them as if a gun had shot spear-sized bullets. The tips of his legs vanished and the new ones grew in a fraction of a second. Before anyone could make out what he exactly did, two spear-like weapons hit the peripheral walls of King Victor's Palace and penetrated through into the waterfalls in the garden. This was just the beginning of wrath that Crato could shower upon anyone who opposed him. He hit the Palace with those Leg-Tips once again and broke the main gates at the entrance.

The people of the kingdom were scared to death but were helpless as there was no alternate place to hide or run. On one side, the soldiers and the General tried to stop Crato's army while on the other side, Crato headed straight towards the castle with no one strong enough to stand against him.

The soldiers deployed outside the Palace aimed their arrows at all parts of Crato and tried to hit him with everything they could, but their arrows had no effect on Crato whatsoever. They then set the tips of their arrows on fire and tried to hit Crato with those, but all of it just made Crato more furious injuring him just a couple of times when he was hit on the head and face. Crato responded with his Leg-Tips back and again killing tens of soldiers with each shot and making his way closer to the entrance. Along with moving forward and attacking the King's Palace, he sprayed a sort of poisonous liquid around through his nostrils and anyone who came in contact with it, died.

And just when nothing else seemed to work, out of the woods and in the way of Crato, appeared Boris. Yes, BORIS!

Crato looked into the eyes of Boris and they immediately reminded him of the legend Yura. With the similar fire in his eyes, and patience to wait for the right time to strike, he held back his nerves and stood between Crato and the castle. Crato now had to think and act, as he was now facing the bloodline of Qahns, which defeated him the last time he invaded.

Not just Crato, even King Victor himself was shocked to see Boris as it was next to impossible to come out of the Forest of Clyssia alive. Princess Zia, however, could not control her happiness on seeing Boris. Everyone was amazed in their own way on seeing Boris back from the forest; Almus, who envied Boris the most, hid behind a rock and witnessed everything quietly from a distance.

A little while ago, when the attack began, Boris ran his lungs out and didn't stop at all in order to return and save his people. Clyssia observed everything taking place and told all the cursed souls living in the forest to be prepared for Boris' help. The Bird, Klaire, Wolfey and Seed-Bearer, all stood at the edge of the forest treeline looking at the fierce battle going in the Kingdom of Ekaardus. By now, Clyssia had conveyed everyone to help Boris in every possible way, even if they had to step out of the forest for that, provided they would return to the forest once the battle was over, if they made it out alive. However, as a part of their plan, all of them stood there, to step out and attack only when they considered it most suitable. Also, Boris left back the Spear of Neutrality with the Seed-Bearer as he didn't want Crato to know that he had found it. Once Crato would see the Spear of Neutrality, he would prepare to save himself from it. Therefore, Boris didn't reveal it and planned to strike with it later.

Back from the shock and into the reality, Crato attacked Boris with his leg-tips but Boris cut all of them with the swings of his sword and remained unhurt and unmoved. Crato then attacked him with the poison but Boris blocked it with his shield which infuriated Crato further. He then jumped close to Boris and started striking with his multiple legs but Boris faced him strongly facing the legs with his sword at times and jumping away from him when needed.

Seeing Boris fighting with Crato alone, King Victor ordered his soldiers to target their arrows on Crato's face and show no mercy on hitting him with everything they got. However, as Crato kept moving randomly while fighting with Boris, he could not be hit as targeted by the soldiers.

Princess Zia could not resist more, and left the Palace riding her horse carrying a sword along with bow and arrows. As she got closer to Crato, she aimed and shot an arrow which hit Crato's eye and wounded him badly. Out of pain, Crato striked Zia back with his leg, throwing her off the horse. Just when Crato's focus diverted from Boris towards Zia, Boris used the opportunity, jumped with immense power and speed towards Crato and with a swing of his sword, cut off Crato's leg once again, which Crato had attached a little while ago.

On the other side of the battlefield, Taantoh could not tackle the General alone and hence, with assistance of his army of beasts, he got successful in injuring the General after which the General could not give further commands to his soldiers leaving them on their own. The soldiers started feeling restless without the commands and instructions and thus started to back-off slowly.

The General, lying wounded, spotted Almus behind a rock and tried to call out to him for help. But Almus had something else on his mind and did not notice his father in pain. Almus had all his focus on Crato's leg that was cut and had fallen apart. On finding the right time, he went ahead and picked up Crato's leg and ran away from the battlefield as quickly as he could. General saw it all like a mute spectator, but could not do anything in the injured condition. That was the last time General would see his son, Almus.

In another part of the Kingdom, the old man Otham continued praying for the Kingdom and its people as he had foreseen that the battle could only be won if Crato was hit by the Spear of Neutrality. However, as that Spear was nowhere to be seen yet, and the General and his soldiers had also lost hope, Otham could only pray to his God for help.

CHAPTER 11

As the morale of soldiers dropped and the General lay injured, Taantoh and his army started moving towards the castle and towards their King Crato who was in pain as well. At that moment, everyone could sense that Boris could not fight them off alone in the absence of soldiers of the Kingdom.

Princess Zia ran close to Boris and stood shoulder-to-shoulder with him irrespective of the whole army of horned-beasts coming towards them. King Victor himself came ahead and stood next to his daughter Zia to face the wrath of Crato together. Queen Alana was in tears seeing everything but showed courage and made sure her people were inside the Palace Hall and safe for as long as she was alive.

While Crato's beasts gathered behind him, the soldiers of Ekaardus moved behind their King, seeking revenge for their deceased fellow warriors. There was no formation, no strategies, no more running or looking back or waiting for the commands or orders; it was the decisive moment when everyone had to give their best to win over the invaders and save their very own land.

Just when their eyes were filled with enough aggression to run for each other's lives once again, another shock wave hit Crato and his army when hundreds of stones and sharp wooden spikes came flying from the Forest of Clyssia and nailed right into the bodies of the beasts. Before anyone could digest what just happened, out from the forest came Wolfey, Klaire and The Bird to attack the invaders. The Seed-Bearer stayed back with the Spear of Neutrality.

The beasts were no longer the stronger army. Stones and spikes bringing them down, a huge muscular wolf charging towards them, an owl-like human flying in the daylight, another huge bird flying low and fast, all of it together brought down

Crato and his army and ofcourse, boosted the courage of King Victor and his soldiers.

Boris nodded his head by looking back towards the soldiers posted on the peripheral wall of King's palace, and they let loose their arrows all at once targeting the army of Crato. As one wave of arrows hit them, King Victor ordered the soldiers behind him in the battlefield to charge ahead and kill the enemies showing no mercy at all. The soldiers reacted as if they were already waiting for the call and ran towards the unwanted invader with their swords thirsty for their blood.

General, although injured badly, gathered back all his courage, stood up and moved towards Taantoh. The Bird, Wolfey and Klaire also pounced at Taantoh all at once. While Wolfey bit his arm off leaving him defenceless with no weapons left, The Bird and Klaire held him from his head and feet respectively and flew high in the air and dropped him off from a height of around 500 feet. Taantoh fell right in front of General and looked into his eyes for the last time breathing heavily. General swung his sword and punched a hole through the chest of Taantoh leaving no scope of his survival.

In the battle, the number of beasts also started decreasing as the spikes from forest and arrows of soldiers, along with the soldiers in the clash tore their bodies apart. Supernatural visions of the Seed-Bearer and Clyssia worked here as well; the arrows and spikes only pierced through the invading army and if any of those reached close to the soldiers of Ekaardus and Xiasha, it fell down on ground before hitting them.

Taantoh dead, and the beasts dying everywhere - it all got next to unbearable for Crato. His madness overtook his senses and he went out of control attacking the opponents altogether. King Victor and Princess Zia fought with a strategy of diverting

Crato's focus in different directions. Both of them jumped to opposite sides and attacked Crato's legs with their sword while Boris remained in front tackling Crato face to face.

Crato could sense that the odds for his victory were diminishing but also knew that he could not be killed with the weapons carried by anyone in that battle. While fighting, he tried to look around for anything that he missed, and that he ought to be extra careful about, but couldn't find anything.

While all of it happened at a fast pace, Boris heard Yura's voice once again:

"Boris, do it, NOW.'

This was the moment when Boris could end all the wrath showered by the King of Seabed, Crato. Boris looked towards the Seed-Bearer and spoke eye to eye which went unnoticed to the rest in the ongoing battle. Along with the rest of the sharp wooden spikes coming out from the forest, the Seed-Bearer threw the Spear of Neutrality towards Boris. The shining unique Spear was easily traceable coming from the forest, but no one noticed it while fighting for their own lives.

King Victor and Zia started swinging their swords more swiftly in order to engage Crato with themselves. Wolfey, Klaire and The Bird also attacked him in order to grab all his attention. Wolfey gripped one of Crato's legs with his jaws while Klaire and The Bird flew around him and hit him with their claws. As the Spear of Neutrality approached closer, Boris threw away his sword and shield and jumped high in the air towards the Spear of Neutrality. Meanwhile, King Victor and Zia wounded a couple of legs and brought immense pain to Crato.

Before anyone could believe and understand the reason behind Boris' flight in the air, he gripped the Spear of Neutrality tightly with both his hands and nailed it into Crato's forehead right between his eyes.

"You don't deserve confinement Crato, you deserve death. Die, Crato, Die." Said Boris while digging the Spear of Neutrality deeper in Crato's head as the King of Seabed lost grip of his legs and fell down hard on the ground.

All the pain, the suffering, the fear, the rage, the panic, the killings, the battle, everything ended with this last daring move of Boris. Crato was grounded with Spear in his head. Taantoh laid with General's sword pierced through his chest. The army of beasts turned to ashes. The ocean went back to normal as well. It all seemed too unreal to believe.

The soldiers of Ekaardus and Xiasha bowed down in front of their new hero, Boris. King Victor did not feel bad about it, he raised his hand looking towards Boris and cheering his soldiers. He walked towards Boris slowly, tired and gaining back his breath. He went close to Boris, called him "The Last Qahn Alive" looking right in his eyes and hugged him tightly laughing in disbelief. While hugging Boris, he looked towards Zia standing at his left and smiled in appreciation of her efforts. Queen Alana rode in her horse cart along with her guards and jumped out of it on reaching close to the King. She ran and hugged the King in happiness of the unbelievable victory, then hugged her daughter tightly and also thanked Boris as it would not have been possible without him.

Once this formal celebration was over with the King and her family, Boris looked towards The Bird, Wolfey and Klaire who were standing together a little distance away. Boris went up to them, thanked them with a smile and asked them if they could stay back for some time.

Klaire responded in her polite tone:

"We were instructed to get back to the forest after the battle, if we survived. Now that we have survived, there is no other option but to return."

Wolfey continued further:

"You have earned immense respect and love of every inch of the forest. Clyssia herself is impressed beyond our capability to put it in words. The trees, the waters, the creatures, the Seed-Bearer, all of us feel proud to be a part of your journey which helped save these innocent people."

The Bird laughed and spoke the final words before leaving:

"Seed-Bearer wants you to know that although he loves you, he won't like to see your face again, as you brought him a lot of trouble (laughing). Also, Clyssia extends her greetings to you, she will be glad if you visit the forest more often, of course alone, as this flexibility is just for you and no one else. And yes, (while looking towards the forest and about to take the flight), we all love you Boris, be the same selfless human always, for this is what makes you stand apart."

With these words, The Bird and Klaire flew towards the forest while Wolfey ran and jumped and disappeared in the trees. Seed-Bearer did not step out, he returned with Wolfey to his own place with the last glimpse of Boris.

CHAPTER 12

As Boris took out the Spear of Neutrality from Crato's body and the General pulled his sword from Taantoh's chest, both of them also turned to ashes and flew with the wind. Boris kept the Spear of Neutrality in his possession just to be on the safer side in case any such attack ever took place again. Wounded General was taken back for healing and was expected to get well in a few days' time.

Just when King Victor was about to ask Boris to come along to the Palace, nomads shouted out for Boris and came running to meet their boy. Boris was happy to see them, although upset for their leader's death but still glad that the others were alive and fine. King Victor asked Boris to join them in Palace, to which Boris requested him for one day which he wanted to spend with his people i.e. Nomads. King happily agreed to that. Queen Alana walked up to Boris and told him to join them for the next day's breakfast as they would all wait eagerly for his presence. Zia just looked at Boris and smiled, she wanted to talk but couldn't as her parents were around.

Next day, after breakfast, Boris was asked to marry Zia by both the King and the Queen, an offer which could not be denied of course. Everyone accepted Boris as their new Prince with all the happiness and appreciation.

After a week, when everything was brought back to normal, all of them were having breakfast together again. General was fine and joined the King's family breakfast as well. Now, out of curiosity, King Victor spoke to General:

"General, I was thinking that because your son brought to your knowledge everything you told me before the banishment of Boris, we shall call him to the palace and ask why he said so. Now that we know all of it was false, the reason for his lie must be asked as well."

After saying this, King Victor told Boris why he was sent to the forest as he was unaware of it all.

General became uneasy on these orders of his King. General knew that Almus had run away with Crato's leg and was not traceable. But no one else knew about it. As he couldn't explain or justify this behaviour of his son, he thought it would be better to keep it hidden, and responded in fear:

"My King, I last met him before the battle. After it was over, he was nowhere to be seen, neither dead nor alive. I am worried for him, and trying to find him."

General's answer increased everyone's doubt on Almus but the confusion remained intact why he lied. Boris and Zia also recalled when they last saw Almus and the suspicious look and smile he carried when they saw him. The fact that he had disappeared worried them more, as his intentions could not be trusted at all.

Everyone finished their breakfast. King Victor and Queen Alana walked towards the garden, while Boris and Zia set-off for their horses to give a round in the Kingdom.

People of the Kingdoms of Ekaardus and Xiasha thus lived happy and safe, not expecting any such invasion again.

CHAPTER 13

No one knew the fate of Ekaardus, and how much more it was bound to endure.

Far away in barren lands, Almus sat alone carrying Crato's leg as his only companion. He knew he would be asked questions after the battle to which he would have no satisfactory answers, that was why he thought of serving Crato from then onwards and left the Kingdom of Ekaardus with Crato's leg.

His initial plan was to wait till the end of the battle and join as Crato's follower when he won. However, that didn't happen and hence, he was left with no other option but to flee from there.

Looking towards Crato's leg through the cloth covering his face, he murmured:

"We will conquer Ekaardus, my King. Soon. Very soon."

Made in the USA
Columbia, SC
22 July 2021